Just George

The favourite character from

Enid Blyton's
Famous Five

George, Timmy and the Curious Treasure

D0242979

*The **Just George** series*
by Sue Welford

Just George

The favourite character from
Enid Blyton's
Famous Five

George, Timmy and the Curious Treasure

Sue Welford

Illustrated by Lesley Harker

Hodder
Children's
Books

a division of Hodder Headline

Copyright © 2000 The Enid Blyton Company
Enid Blyton's signature is a Registered Trade Mark of
Enid Blyton Ltd.
All rights reserved
Illustrations © 2000 Lesley Harker

First published in Great Britain in 2000
by Hodder Children's Books

10 9 8 7 6 5 4 3 2 1

The right of Sue Welford to be identified as the Author of
the Work has been asserted by her in accordance with the
Copyright, Designs and Patents Act 1988.

For further information on Enid Blyton,
please contact www.blyton.com

A Catalogue record for this book is available from
the British Library

ISBN 0 340 77864 4

Typeset by Avon Dataset Ltd, Bidford-on-Avon, Warks

Printed and bound in Great Britain by
The Guernsey Press Co. Ltd, Channel Isles

Hodder Children's Books
A division of Hodder Headline Ltd
338 Euston Road
London NW1 3BH

Contents

1

Timothy is naughty

'Timmy will be good, honestly, Father,' cried George, gazing up at her tall, rather stern parent. '*Please* let him stay!'

It had been a whole month since George, a little girl with very short, dark curly hair and vivid blue eyes, had found the stray puppy on the moor behind her house. She had asked

everywhere to see if she could find the shaggy brown puppy's owner but no-one had come forward. The village policeman had told her that if he was not claimed within a month he would have to be found a new home. Now the month was up and George could not bear to be parted from him. She had been allowed to keep the puppy at home and he had become her best friend. They went everywhere together and she had even named him – Timothy.

Now it was time to decide Timothy's future and George's father was looking uncertain.

'He did chew my best slippers,' said the tall man, gazing down at his small daughter. He was very dark and extraordinary-looking with blue eyes and thick brows that frowned a lot. Exactly like George.

Father and daughter both had quick tempers and often quarrelled even though they loved one another dearly.

'But you know Timmy's only a puppy, Father,' declared George when her father mentioned the chewed slippers. 'He'll get better as he gets older.'

'And he's done puddles in the kitchen, twice,' said Father, still with a deep, dark frown on his face.

'Well, if you won't let him stay then I won't stay either,' said George angrily, trying her best *not* to lose her temper but not succeeding very well. 'He's my best friend and I won't let him go to another home. He'd hate it. Wouldn't you Timmy, darling?' she said, bending to hug the little dog.

'Wuff,' said Timothy sadly. He could not bear to think of being parted from his beloved mistress.

'If you made friends with some of the girls in the village,' continued George's father, 'you wouldn't be lonely and need to have a dog as your best friend.'

'I'm not at all lonely,' declared George, her face going red with annoyance. 'And Timmy is the only friend I need.'

George was not like ordinary little girls. She wanted more than anything to be a boy and hated her real name of Georgina. In fact, if anyone called her that, she simply would not

4

answer them. She always dressed in shorts and a shirt and her face, arms and legs were as brown as a hazelnut from playing out in the sunshine. She could sail and fish and climb trees, whistle and run as fast as any boy. She had even cut off her long hair so she would *look* like a boy. Boys, thought George, are much, much better than silly, babyish girls and puppies are even better!

'Wuff,' agreed Timothy, when he heard George say he was the only friend she needed. He gazed up at his small, angry mistress with his big, melting brown eyes. He thumped his shaggy tail on the floor.

'He knows every word she's saying,' said George's mother with a sigh as she came into the room. 'Really, Quentin, I think you should let the dog stay. I've got quite fond of the little chap.'

'Thanks, Mummy,' said George, giving her mother a grateful glance.

'Oh, very well, Fanny,' said George's father irritably to his wife. 'But you *must* keep him quiet and not let him chew anything else.

Do you understand, Georgina?'

George scowled once again. Why did Father always forget she hated that name? But this time she was too full of happiness to be angry for more than a few seconds. The scowl quickly disappeared. She flung her arms round her father's waist and hugged him as hard as could be.

'Oh, thank you, Father,' she cried, her eyes shining with joy.

'Wurf,' said Timothy, jumping up at her, his tail wagging nineteen to the dozen. George let her father go and scooped the puppy up in her arms. *'He's* saying thank you too,' she said, laughing.

Father patted Timothy's soft head. 'Now, mind you behave yourself,' he said, turning to go out of the door and along to his study at the other end of the house. He was working on an important scientific formula and intended writing a book about the results. 'And no noise!' he called as he went in and banged the door shut.

'Oh, Mummy isn't that marvellous?' cried

George, still hugging Timothy so tightly that the little dog could hardly breathe. 'I can keep him at Kirrin Cottage for ever and ever!'

Kirrin Cottage was the name of the old white stone house where the family lived. It was really too big to be called a cottage. It had an old wooden front door, a beautiful red rose growing up the wall and a garden full of flowers.

The house was set on top of a low cliff overlooking Kirrin Bay. Guarding the entrance to the bay was a little rocky island called Kirrin Island. On the island was a mysterious ruined castle with two tumbledown towers and a stone courtyard. George loved to play on the island amongst the wild rabbits and flocks of seagulls. She often rowed there in her little wooden boat. She adored the castle with its ruined walls that once stood strong and proud overlooking the sea, and loved playing in the towers and the old room with its ancient stone fireplace. She imagined all the exciting things that could have happened there in days gone by. She would often pretend she was a knight or a soldier

defending Kirrin Bay from deadly enemies.

The cottage and the island had belonged to her mother's family for many years. None of them could imagine living anywhere else in the world.

'Right,' said George's mother when the little girl had finished hugging Timothy and put him back down on the carpet. Straightaway the naughty puppy began biting and growling at the laces of George's plimsolls. Biting shoelaces was one of his favourite games. 'That's settled then,' continued her mother, laughing at the puppy. 'Now dear, I want you to do something for me.'

'What's that, Mummy?' asked George, giggling and moving out of Timothy's way.

'I've promised to send some things to the village jumble sale. I'd like you to go up in the attic and turn out some of your old toys,' said her mother. 'I've already found some old things that I've put in the garden shed. You can add your toys to the pile.'

'Very well,' said George, prising the puppy's teeth gently from her laces. 'Come on, Timmy, let's see what we can find.'

'Your father is working,' called Mother as the two ran helter-skelter up the stairs. 'So don't make too much noise!'

2

A strange find

'This is going to be great fun, Timmy,' said George, pushing open the little, low door that led into the attic. The attic at Kirrin Cottage was set under the sloping roof at the far end of the house and the door was so small that even George had to bend down to get through.

Timothy followed. This was a very interesting

room he hadn't been in before. He ran round between the old wooden rafters hunting for smells. There were lots of different ones, all new and exciting.

First the little dog could smell spiders and ran round in between dusty suitcases and boxes packed with old clothes trying to find where they were.

There were some tremendous mouse smells too. Timothy's sharp nose caught the scent of birds and beetles and lots of interesting things. This was one of the most thrilling places he had ever set his paws in!

'Over here, Timmy,' called George as she pulled out a trunk full of old toys that had belonged to her when she was a lot smaller.

She opened the lid and looked inside. There were some old toy cars and a train set she hadn't played with for ages. There were some picture books too and several old jigsaw puzzles and a box full of wooden building bricks.

'Oh, Timmy, here's my old football!' she cried, holding up a rather sorry-looking leather ball that was flat as a pancake. 'I remember it got a puncture and Father was too busy to ever mend it.'

'Wuff,' said Timothy, thinking that a flat old football wouldn't be much good for a proper game.

George brought out something else and held it up. 'And here's my cowboy outfit that I grew out of. I'm sure some little boy will be pleased to buy it at the sale.' She put it to one side to take down to her mother.

Then George came across a cardboard box and opened it. Inside was a doll with blonde hair and dressed in a pink satin frock. 'Ugh!' she cried, screwing up her nose. 'This can go to the jumble sale, Timmy, that's for sure!'

The doll had been sent to George one Christmas by an aunt and uncle who lived in London. The aunt and uncle had three children who were George's cousins. Their names were Julian, Dick and Anne. George had never met them and did not particularly want to. Especially as one of them was a girl!

'My cousin Anne probably likes dolls and

Aunt must have thought I liked them too,' said George to Timothy, who was staring at the doll as if he would like to grab it and shake it hard between his sharp little teeth. 'That just shows what she knows about *me*!' she added haughtily, putting the doll on top of the cowboy outfit.

'Wuff,' said Timothy, agreeing as usual.

Soon there was quite a pile of things for the sale. George looked around for something to put them in. She spotted a large, empty cardboard box and went to fetch it. In the bottom was a scrap of old newspaper, tattered and yellow and rather cobwebby. A word written on the torn headline caught her sharp eyes.

'Detectives Hunt for Bones,' she read out loud to Timothy. 'A search is taking place in Kirrin Bay for . . .' she stopped and gave a sigh. 'The rest of the story is missing,' she said, turning to the puppy with a sparkle in her vivid blue eyes. 'Detectives in Kirrin Bay, though. How exciting, Timmy!'

She turned over the ragged piece of newspaper but there was only an advertisement on the other side. The date was years and years ago.

'Oh, well,' said the little girl. 'I suppose we'll never know the rest of the story.' She screwed up the paper and threw it away. 'Come on, Timmy. Let's get this stuff down to Mummy, then we can go out for a walk.'

'Wuff,' said Timothy excitedly. '*Walk*' was another word he knew very well indeed!

When George showed her mother the box of toys, she was very pleased. 'I'm sure the organisers will be delighted,' she said. 'Thank you, George. It's such a lovely day, why don't you take Timmy out along the beach?'

'All right, Mummy,' said George. Then she had an exciting idea. 'I know, Timmy, let's have a picnic!'

'Wuff,' said Timothy, his big ears pricking upright. He loved picnics. Joanna, the woman who cooked for the family and helped George's mother in the house, made wonderful cakes and pies. If he was very good he might be allowed to have some. A picnic sounded a marvellous idea.

'Go into the kitchen and ask Joanna to make you some sandwiches,' said George's mother.

'Come on, Tim,' said George. 'We'll go for a swim too if you like.'

'Wuff,' barked Timothy joyfully. If there was one thing he liked beside walks, bones and picnics, it was splashing around in the warm waters of Kirrin Bay.

In the kitchen, Joanna was making a batch of bread. It smelled delicious and George's mouth watered as she ran in with Timothy at her heels.

'Mmm, Joanna!' she exclaimed, eyeing two warm freshly baked loaves on the kitchen table. 'Could you make me some sandwiches with that lovely bread? Timmy and I are going to have a picnic.'

'A picnic? Oh, well, I should think so,' said Joanna with a smile. She was a round woman with a jolly face. 'What else would you like to go with them?' The pantry at Kirrin Cottage was always full of delicious things to make picnics with.

'Oh, some of your luscious apple pie and home-made lemonade,' cried George. 'And

some cheese, and some of Mummy's ripe tomatoes to go with the bread, please ... ooh, and some plums from the garden too.'

'Right you are,' said Joanna, laughing and bustling about getting the picnic ready.

'And please may Timmy have some of his biscuits and a bone?' called George over her shoulder as she ran upstairs to get her swimming costume and a towel.

Soon the picnic was ready. Joanna had packed it in George's rucksack. George stuffed her swimming things in too and hitched it up on her back. She ran outside into the fresh air. Timothy scampered after her, his tail waving in the air like a banner. He had sniffed all the goodies going into the rucksack and couldn't wait for picnic time. This was going to be tremendous fun!

3

Timothy goes digging

Down the garden the little girl and her puppy went on their way to the beach. Skipping past the old apple tree where George had built a tree-house high up in the branches. Past the garden shed and Mother's flower-beds and vegetable patch. And through the gate that led to the cliff path.

The path led down to the bay. Down they went, Timothy scampering on ahead sniffing for rabbits and birds and anything else interesting that might have passed that way.

George stuck her hands in the pockets of her shorts. She whistled a merry tune and thought how lucky she was to live so close to the sea and have such a lovely friend as Timothy to play with.

It was a lovely sunny day as the two ran down the path to the shore. White fluffy clouds drifted across a blue sky and the air was full of birdsong and the buzzing of insects in the heather.

Kirrin Bay was a wide, curved stretch of golden sand, shining in the bright sunlight. Little waves broke on the shore with hardly a murmur. A flock of seagulls wheeled and dived in the clear air. George took a deep breath. She loved the bay and the island. They really were the best places in the whole wide world.

They soon found a good place in the shelter of a large rock to have their picnic. George shrugged off her rucksack and quickly made a hollow in the warm sand. She sat down inside it, staring out at Kirrin Island. She felt the sun warming her skin and smelled the wonderful scent of the sea.

Timothy sat beside her for a minute or two. Then he jumped up and rushed, barking, down the beach chasing a flock of seagulls that had landed close to the water's edge.

'Don't chase the birds, Timothy!' shouted George sternly. 'You know I've told you that before!' She loved all the seabirds and didn't want Timothy scaring them away.

The puppy came back to her looking rather sorry for himself. He *knew* he wasn't allowed to chase them. Somehow, though, he just couldn't help it. He didn't really know what his dear mistress was worried about. He never, ever caught one. In fact, he became very annoyed when they flew off out of his reach. How was a puppy supposed to catch things that flew so high in the air?

George grinned at him and gave him a hug. 'Sorry, darling Tim, but you know you mustn't do it,' she said.

21

'Wurf,' Timothy said, as if to apologise.

'Sit down here, there's a good boy,' said George, patting the sand beside her. 'It's so lovely and warm.'

When Timothy was sitting down beside her, she unpacked her rucksack. She took out the packet of sandwiches and opened one up. Joanna had put cheese and pickle inside. Her very favourite, especially if eaten with home-grown tomatoes. She gave Timothy a handful of biscuits. The puppy soon crunched and

chewed his way through them and watched George enviously as she munched away at her sandwiches. Joanna's bread tasted as delicious as it had smelled.

When George had finished the sandwiches she gave Timothy a piece of crust, then ate her slice of apple pie. She washed it down with a swig of lemonade straight from the bottle. It tasted much better that way. She rounded off her feast with two juicy red plums from the garden, then tried to see how far she could spit out the stones.

One of the stones went right to the water's edge.

'Brilliant, don't you think, Timmy?' laughed George. 'I bet I can spit further than any boy in the world.'

'Wurf,' agreed Timothy, even though he thought spitting stones seemed to be rather a silly thing to do. Chasing gulls was much more fun.

'Mmm, Timmy, I'm really full up,' said the little girl, giving a sigh of contentment.

She lay down in her sand hollow with her

face up to the sun. Timothy lay beside her, his head between his paws, staring longingly at the seagulls.

'We'll go for a swim when our picnic has gone down,' said George, knowing it was not wise to swim directly after eating. 'Then we'll have a lovely splash about.'

Half an hour later, she jumped up. 'I'm going for a swim now, Timmy,' she said. 'Coming?' She quickly stripped off her shorts and shirt and put on her costume. Timothy barked with excitement and ran with her to the edge of the water. George dived in. She was a very fast, very strong swimmer for a little girl of her age and could hold her breath underwater for ages.

Timothy was still too little to swim so he paddled and splashed about close to the edge for a while then came out and sat waiting patiently for George as she swum strongly up and down like a little seal.

Something caught the puppy's eye and he wandered off away from the edge of the waves. He sniffed around behind one of the rocks. It was a very tall pointed rock called Needle Rock.

His plumy tail wagged with excitement. There was a very interesting smell here that he had not come across before!

By the time George came out of the water Timothy had dug quite a deep hole for such a small puppy. George shook the water from her eyes and ran to get her towel. As she quickly dried herself, she noticed Timothy's rear end sticking out of the hole, his tail waving like a flag.

'Timmy! What *are* you up to?' she laughed, running over to see what was going on.

Timothy came out backwards and shook a whole shower of sand out of his shaggy coat. She saw he had something in his mouth.

'What *have* you found?' cried the little girl in amazement, for, lying in front of Timothy, was a large bone. It was long and thick and had strange-looking knobs at one end although the other end was broken and jagged.

George gave a gasp of surprise. She picked up the bone and stared at it. 'Timmy!' she exclaimed. 'Fancy finding a bone buried in Kirrin Bay. However did it get here?'

Then she suddenly remembered the torn piece of newspaper she had found in the loft back at Kirrin Cottage. *Detectives Search for Bones*! She looked at Timothy excitedly. 'Oh, Timmy,' she cried. 'Have we found one of the bones the detectives were searching for, do you think?'

'Wuff,' said Timothy, wondering how long it would be before his small mistress gave him back his bone so he could start chewing it.

'I think we'd better take it home straight-away,' said George. 'I don't know *what* Mummy and Father are going to say when they see it!'

4

Father's strange reaction

'What on earth have you got there?' exclaimed George's mother as they came through the gate and into the garden with the bone Timothy had dug from the sand.

George was quite red in the face from hurrying back up the cliff path to the cottage.

'A bone,' said George, pulling it out of her

rucksack. It had been sticking out of the top as it was far too long to fit inside.

'That's odd,' said Mother, gazing at it with a frown on her face. 'Where did you find it?'

'Timmy dug it up on the beach near Needle Rock,' explained George. She went close to her mother and gazed up at her. 'Do you think it's a *human* bone?' she said in a low voice.

'Oh, I don't really think so, darling,' laughed her mother kindly. 'What would a human bone be doing buried in our dear Kirrin Bay?'

'Well, I—' began George but she was interrupted by her father coming out of the back door looking for his wife.

'Fanny!' called the tall man. 'What time does the train go again?'

'Father's going up to London,' explained Mother. 'I'd better go and write down the train times otherwise he'll probably forget them altogether.' She handed the bone back to George and hurried indoors.

George and Timothy followed her. Father had gone back to his study. He had forgotten to wait for his wife to tell him what time the train left.

'I'm going to show him the bone, Timmy,' said George, hurrying after him. 'He'll know all about it, I'm sure!' She ran along the hall and knocked on the study door.

'Who is it?' came an irritable voice from inside. 'I'm busy.'

'You can't be busy, Father,' said George, opening the door and going in. 'You're supposed to be going to catch the train to London.'

'Am I?' said Father, looking up from his note-book. George could see the pages were covered with very important formulas. 'Oh yes, of course I am.' George's father was very absent-minded and often forgot things. He shut the book with a bang and put it in his briefcase. 'What did you want, George? I've got to go in a minute.'

George held up the bone. 'Do you know what kind of a bone this is, Father?' Timothy tried to jump up and grab it. 'Down!' she commanded sternly.

Timothy sat down looking rather hurt. After all it was *his* bone. He had been the one to dig it up.

George's father stared very hard at the bone, then took it from her. 'Where on earth did you find this, George?' he asked, frowning deeply.

'Timmy dug it up on the beach,' answered the little girl. 'Don't you think it's strange, Father?'

'Very,' said Father, suddenly sounding very excited. He stroked his chin, his dark eyes gleaming. 'Very strange and rather marvellous, I think. I'll take it up to London with me and show it to a friend of mine. My word, George, I've got a feeling this bone could be very important! Very important indeed!'

Then George's father did something very unusual. He bent down and gave Timothy a hug and a pat. 'Well *done*, Timmy! Good boy!' he exclaimed.

'Don't you think you should tell the police?' asked George, feeling rather puzzled at her father's strange behaviour.

Father stared at her. 'Police? Don't be silly, George,' he said. 'This bone is far too old for them to be interested in.'

'But—' she began. But she didn't get any

further as her father picked up his briefcase, pushed past and hurried out of the room.

The two followed. Father took his coat and hat from the hallstand and opened the front door. 'Goodbye, Fanny,' he called. 'I'll see you tomorrow.'

The last George saw of him was as he walked briskly out of the front gate and down the road towards the railway station. Mother ran after him and gave him the train times she had written down. He stuffed the piece of paper into his pocket, kissed her quickly, then hurried off again. He looked most peculiar with a large bone in one hand and his briefcase in the other.

Mother came back to the house looking puzzled. 'Why has Quentin taken that bone with him?' she asked George.

'I've no idea,' said George, feeling annoyed. 'It was Timmy's bone and he just took it away without even asking permission.'

'But what is he going to *do* with it?' asked her mother, still looking rather puzzled.

'He said he's going to show it to a friend of his,' said George.

'Oh, well, never mind, dear,' said Mother patting George's dark curls. 'I'm sure Father knows what he's doing.'

'I hope so,' said George with a sigh. She bent to give Timothy a hug. 'Sorry, Tim, it looks as if you've lost your bone for the time being.'

What could have been an exciting and mysterious adventure had turned out to be rather a damp squib after all.

George and Timothy wandered out into the garden. George stood under the apple tree gazing up at her tree-house. She had been racking her brains for a way to get Timothy up there. Joanna's husband William, who sometimes helped Mother in the garden, had made a ladder but she couldn't climb up carrying the dog. She did try once but he wriggled and she was afraid she might drop him.

Timothy sat and stared at the tree-house too. He was longing to get up there and explore for any exciting smells.

'Wuff,' he said sadly.

George bent down and gave him another

hug. 'Never mind, Tim, we'll think of a way of getting you up there, don't worry.'

When she went indoors Mother was standing in the hall with Father's small suitcase in her hand.

'Your father's forgotten to take his night things,' she said with a sigh. 'One day he'll forget his own head.'

George giggled at the thought of her father

running for the train with a bone and a brief-case but no head!

That evening there was a telephone call from him. George was reading her adventure comic in the lounge when the phone rang.

'Very well, Quentin,' she heard her mother say. 'I'll get the spare rooms ready. About midday? Yes, very well. Goodbye, dear.'

George's mother put the phone down and came into the lounge. 'We're having visitors, George,' she said. 'They're coming with Father tomorrow.'

'Visitors!' exclaimed George, looking up from her comic. 'Oh, blow! I hate visitors!'

'Well, that's too bad, dear,' said her mother. 'Your father's bringing his friend back from London to stay for a few days, so I hope you'll be polite and not scowl at him all the time.'

'What is he coming here for?' asked George curiously.

'He's very excited about that bone you found and he wants you to show him exactly where Timmy dug it up,' said her mother.

'The tide will have washed away the hole,'

said George. 'But I suppose we can still find the place, if we have to, can't we, Tim, darling?'

'Wuff,' said Timothy. He was rather puzzled about all the fuss being made about a bone. He had always thought it was *dogs* who became excited about bones, not humans!

5

Visitors!

'Who *is* Father's friend?' asked George curiously when her mother announced they were to have visitors. 'Is he a detective?' She thought perhaps a policeman was coming to find out about the bone Timothy had dug out of the sand.

'Don't be silly, dear,' said her mother. 'Your

father's friends are all scientists, like him.'

That was twice people had told George not to be silly when she'd mentioned policemen. She thought she had better not mention them again. She hated grown-ups telling her she was being silly when most of the time it was *them* who were being silly.

'Father's friend is a palaeontologist,' explained her mother.

'A *what*?' asked George who was not very good at knowing what long words meant.

'He studies old bones and fossils,' said her mother patiently. 'He's a sort of bone professor.'

George screwed up her nose. Studying bones seemed a very peculiar thing to do. Unless you were a dog, of course.

'Does he want to study the bone Timmy found, then?' asked George.

'Apparently,' said her mother. 'And he also wants to see if he can find any more like it. Oh, and by the way he's bringing his son with him.'

'His son!' exclaimed George.

'Yes,' said her mother. 'So I want you to be nice to him, George. They live in the city and aren't used to life in the country so you'll have to be very patient and kind.'

'Patient and kind!' exclaimed George. 'Is he a baby, then?' She felt very angry and upset. She really didn't want any city boy staying at Kirrin Cottage. She and Timmy were having such a lovely time. A city boy would spoil everything!

'No, of course he isn't. He's about your age, I believe,' said Mother. 'It'll be nice for you to have someone to play with.'

'I've *got* someone to play with,' said George, flinging down her comic. 'I've got Timmy and I don't want anyone else, thank you very much, Mummy!'

She stormed out of the room with Timothy scampering behind her. He didn't know why his little mistress was so upset. After all, the visitor *could* have been a girl. George would have hated *that* even more!

George strode through the kitchen and out of the back door, slamming it hard behind her. She went to her garden swing and sat on it, moodily swinging to and fro. Trust Father to ruin the holidays for her. She would have to be friendly

and polite to people she didn't even know. It was just too bad!

Father and the visitors arrived at noon the following day. Joanna had been busy since very early morning making cakes and pies for them, washing lettuces and tomatoes from the garden and baking a huge batch of fresh bread.

'Boys have enormous appetites,' she said when George was giving Timothy his breakfast.

'So have girls,' said George indignantly. 'Especially ones like me!'

'That's true,' said Joanna, smiling broadly at the little tomboy.

George's mother was bustling about, going up and down the stairs with armfuls of clean sheets and blankets. George decided to keep out of the way, so she took Timothy for a very long walk on the moor. She was still angry at the thought of having a stranger to stay. She had always been on her own and had grown rather selfish. She loved sharing things with Timothy but sharing with another person was different altogether.

It was cool and drizzly that morning as George and Timothy set off. Grey clouds loomed overhead and the bushes were festooned with raindrops.

Timothy scampered on ahead, his shaggy coat picking up drops of rain as he ran along.

Up the narrow path they went, between wild strips of scratchy heather. This was the place where George had found Timothy, crouching in the undergrowth, alone and scared.

Today though, the puppy was with his beloved mistress and he trotted along happily, sniffing for rabbits and hedgehogs.

George walked with her head down, muttering to herself and kicking at the stones with the toe of her Wellington boot. 'Visitors! That's spoiled all our adventures now, Timmy, you wait and see.'

She put Timothy on his lead and went as close to the cliff edge as she dared. On the horizon the sun was just peeping through the clouds and sending bright pathways down to the sea. Behind them, the drizzly sky was rolling away. It was going to be a lovely day after all.

George sat down, not minding about the damp grass. Timothy lay down beside her and rested his head on her lap. 'Oh, well, Tim,' she said with a sigh. 'The sun's going to come out after all. I suppose it won't be *too* bad having the bone professor to stay. And I suppose it *might* be fun having a boy to make friends with.'

Timothy gave a little whine and wagged his tail very hard. He gazed up at George from under his shaggy eyebrows. 'Wuff,' he said and licked her hand. He was pleased his mistress was feeling more cheerful.

'Darling Tim!' said George laughing and giving him a hug. 'I knew you'd agree!' She got to her feet, suddenly feeling a lot better. 'Come on, let's get home.'

Safely away from the cliff edge, George let the puppy off his lead again. He bounced on ahead, running back the way they had come. The sun had come out now and steam rose from the damp ground. The sea sparkled and the sky was a vivid blue. It really was too nice to be miserable.

When she arrived back at Kirrin Cottage, George saw at once that the visitors had arrived. Joanna was setting lunch out on the lawn and George could hear voices through the French windows. She stood in the doorway shuffling her feet.

'Georgina and Timmy will be back shortly and they'll show you round,' she heard her mother say.

'*Georgina!*' hissed George to Timothy, scowling fiercely. 'Why is she calling me *that*?'

Someone replied from the other side of the room. The person was hidden by the long curtains that framed the doorway.

'It's rather too hot to do *anything*,' the voice said in a kind of whining tone. 'I shan't want to go out in the sun, it's awfully bad for you, you know.'

'I'm afraid Georgina plays outside all the time,' said Mother. 'She's as brown as a berry.'

'Perhaps Timmy will stay in with me, then,' said the voice. 'I don't know much about girls anyway, to be honest. There are only boys at my school, you see.'

George giggled. The bone professor's son thought Timmy was a *boy*! What fun!

'Will you be helping your father dig for the bones, Jack?' asked George's father, not bothering to explain about Timothy, if he had indeed even noticed what the boy had said.

'Not if it's this hot,' came the cross voice again.

Goodness, thought George. That boy sounds

as grumpy as I am sometimes!

The curtain must have twitched because Father called out. 'Is that you, George? For goodness sake stop lurking out there and come in and meet our guests!'

6

Clever Timmy!

Reluctantly, George stepped into the room to meet the visitors.

Timmy ran in front of her, wagging his tail. He really was a very friendly little dog. The bone professor was standing in front of the fireplace. He was short and fat with a large head. He wore a rather crumpled-looking suit with a bright red shirt underneath. George had never seen anyone wearing a shirt *quite* that colour before. He also wore a battered-looking straw hat tilted to one side. George didn't think he looked a bit like a professor!

The professor's son, Jack, was lolling in the armchair. He was short and rather fat too. He wore small, steel-rimmed spectacles and peered at George over the top of them like a shiny-faced owl.

'Hello, young lady,' boomed the bone professor. 'Come in, come in, let's have a look at you.'

'I'm not a young lady,' said George, scowling. This seemed to be a very bad start. Anyone who called George a young lady was in her bad books straightaway!

The bone professor, whose name was Professor Ward, gave a hearty laugh. 'Oh, well, whatever you are,' he said. 'Come in and tell me exactly where you found that marvellous bone your father brought to show me.'

'Timmy found it, not me,' said George, still scowling. She really couldn't understand quite

what was so wonderful about an old bone. Mysterious, yes. But *marvellous*?

'Where is Timmy, then?' piped up Jack, hoping at least he would have someone to play with.

'He's there, silly,' said George, forgetting to scowl and grinning as Timothy ran across and tried to playfully grab the boy's trouser leg.

'Oh, he's a *dog*,' laughed Jack, his irritable expression disappearing like magic. 'I like dogs.' He bent down and gently pulled Timothy away. 'I thought Tim was your brother!' He stroked the puppy's shaggy coat and gave him a hug.

Timothy wagged his tail and licked Jack's shiny face. Everyone laughed except George. She hated Timothy being friends with anyone but herself. She ran over and picked him up.

'He's better than a brother,' she said. 'He's my best friend.'

'And he'll be my best friend too if he'll show me where he found that bone,' said the professor.

'Wuff, wuff,' said Timothy, struggling to get down. George put him on the floor. He ran to the professor and sat at his feet, looking up and wagging his tail like mad.

'Wurf,' he barked excitedly and everyone laughed again. Except George. She was still scowling. If Timothy was going to like the bone professor and his son better than he liked her, having visitors was going to be worse than she'd thought!

George needn't have worried, though. The friendly puppy soon came back to her and sat by her feet, staring up at her with his big, melting brown eyes. He was only being polite to the visitors. He could never love anyone as much as he loved his small mistress.

Joanna had spread the table with a delicious salad. Fresh lettuce and tomatoes from the garden with smoked ham and potato salad, crisp spring onions and scarlet beetroot. She had baked a plum pie for pudding and made a large jug of creamy custard to go with it. Jack tucked in as if he had not eaten for a week.

George could not help staring at him as he piled large helpings of everything on to his plate. Joanna was right about boys, she thought. They *did* have enormous appetites! She made up her mind there and then to try to eat just as much as he did.

'You see, young lady . . . er, Georgina . . .' began the professor when he had finished his salad.

'George,' said George, her mouth full of potato salad.

'She won't answer to Georgina,' whispered her mother in Professor Ward's ear.

'Oh . . . er . . . sorry,' said the professor. 'Well . . . George, then.'

'That's a boy's name,' said Jack, peering at her from over the top of his glasses and crunching a large mouthful of lettuce. This certainly was a strange family, he thought. A scientist who hardly ever came out of his study, a girl who looked like a boy, and a house in the middle of nowhere. Very strange indeed.

'That's why I like it,' said George, giving him one of her dark stares.

'George, are you going to listen to what the professor has to say?' asked her father sharply. 'Or are we going to spend all day discussing names?'

The professor leaned closer to George. 'George,' he said, smiling. 'The bone that Timmy found was very important indeed.'

'Yes, I know,' said George. 'I knew that detectives were looking for bones ages ago.'

'Detectives?' said Father with a frown. 'What are you talking about, George?'

George explained about the torn newspaper she had found in the loft.

Her father frowned and scratched his chin for a moment. 'I don't remember anything like that taking place,' he said, looking most puzzled.

'It must have been when the first old bone was found,' said his wife, laughing. 'Oh, George dear, no wonder you thought Father should tell the police. I remember the newspaper story now. It said *Dinosaur Detectives Hunt for Bones*.'

'I thought *detectives* meant policemen!'

exclaimed George, feeling a bit silly.

Everyone laughed so loudly that George went red and scowled round at everybody. It wasn't *her* fault the newspaper had been torn and tattered.

'Trust a *girl* to think that,' said Jack scornfully, laughing louder than anyone.

George gave him one of her extra special glares. He really was horrible. How was she

going to bear him staying at Kirrin Cottage? Worse still, when Jack laughed, Timothy ran over to him and jumped up, barking excitedly. Jack made a great fuss of him and, much to George's annoyance, Timothy seemed to like him very much.

'Come *here*, Timothy!' she called sternly. 'Now stay here,' she insisted as the puppy trotted back to her side. He sat down and looked up at her. He couldn't understand why she was angry with him. He was only being friendly.

'An easy mistake to make,' said Professor Ward kindly about George's misunderstanding. 'Now, George, let me explain. Several years ago someone found a fragment of dinosaur bone on the beach in Kirrin Bay.'

Dinosaurs! The scowl disappeared from George's face. Things were suddenly becoming *much* more interesting. Prehistoric animals were very thrilling indeed. 'I didn't know anything about that!' she exclaimed.

'It was before you were born,' explained her mother gently.

'There was great excitement,' continued the professor. 'Because the bone belonged to a type of prehistoric animal that was completely unknown to science.'

'Golly!' exclaimed George. 'Kirrin Bay must have been jolly famous then.'

'Yes, it was for a while,' said her mother. 'But although lots of people came here to search, no more bones were ever found.'

'Until Timothy found one,' added Father.

'Well,' said George, giving the puppy a hug. 'He *is* the cleverest dog in the world, you know.'

'Yes, I can see that,' said the bone professor with a smile. 'And I'm hoping that we can now find the whole skeleton. Wouldn't that be thrilling?'

'Yes,' said George thoughtfully. 'But it would be horrid if you dug up the whole of Kirrin Bay.'

'Oh, no, I promise you we won't do that,' said the professor, smiling again. 'If I think the site is interesting I'll get a team together to recover the rest of the bones. When we've finished I promise you your lovely bay will look just the same as it ever did.'

'Good,' said George.

When they had all finished eating, the professor stood up. 'Now,' he said eagerly. 'Shall we all go down to the bay?'

7

More bones

'I'm not coming,' said Jack, when his father suggested they all went down to the beach. 'I'll stay here with Timmy. I can't think of anything worse than tramping along a hot beach in the hot sunshine.'

'Oh, no, you won't,' said George, giving the boy another black look. 'Timmy comes everywhere with me!'

'I think you should let him stay just for once,' said her mother hastily. 'After all, Jack *is* our guest.'

'I don't care,' said George defiantly, calling Timothy and going out into the garden. 'He's not staying here! If Jack wants to play with him he'll have to come with the rest of us.'

She didn't really *want* the boy to go with them but she certainly wasn't leaving Timothy behind!

Jack gave a sigh and got up out of the chair. 'Oh, all right, then,' he said, following her out. 'But if the heat makes me ill, it'll be your fault.'

'Ill!' snorted George. She had thought girls were weak and babyish. Now it was jolly obvious that some boys were too!

Father gave a sigh as he came out with the professor. 'I'm afraid my daughter can be rather rude at times,' he said.

If anyone tries to take Timmy away from me, thought George, I can be a lot ruder than that!

So down to Kirrin Bay everyone went on a bone hunt. Father, Mother and the professor, the edges of his jacket flapping in the breeze and his hat tilted jauntily to one side.

George ran on ahead with Timothy bounding by her side.

'Dinosaurs, Timmy!' said the little girl excitedly to her puppy friend. 'They're enormous! Can you imagine them living at Kirrin Bay?'

Timothy barked as if to say, 'I wouldn't care *how* big they were. I'd bark and bark until they ran away!'

Last of all came Jack. He squinted in the bright sun and lagged behind. He looked very hot and bothered indeed as they crossed the sand towards the place where Timothy had found the dinosaur bone. George could see that the walk to the shore had been worse than Jack had imagined. She supposed it must be very difficult to walk on the sand when you had only been used to hard pavements. The sun was beating down on his head like a hot iron and he looked completely out of breath already.

'Who does that island belong to?' panted the boy when he caught up with the others.

'Me,' replied George.

'Don't be silly.' Jack screwed up his eyes as he stared out towards Kirrin Island. 'How can a girl own an island?'

'Well, it's *almost* mine,' said George. 'It belongs to Mummy and she's promised to give it to me one day. And the castle will be mine too!'

'A likely story,' Jack said disbelievingly, going to sit in the shade of one of the big rocks. 'I'm staying here.' He flopped down with a sigh and wiped his face with his handkerchief.

'I don't care if you don't believe me. It's true, so there!' said George indignantly, running on ahead to catch up with the others.

They all stopped close to Needle Rock. 'Now, George,' said Professor Ward. 'Can you show me exactly where the little fellow found it?'

'Show them, Timmy,' said George and the puppy ran round the rock. Straightaway he began digging again. Showers of sand and shingle flew up into the air.

The professor followed and caught hold of the puppy's collar, hauling him gently away. 'Good boy!' he said. 'Good boy, Timmy!'

Timothy's tail wagged nineteen to the dozen. This was excellent fun but rather puzzling. If he dug holes in the garden he was told off. Now someone was *praising* him for digging. What funny things humans were!

George held him back while the professor knelt down and examined the hole closely. He didn't seem to notice that the knees of his trousers were getting damp and sandy. He picked something up and took a magnifying glass from his pocket, peering at it closely.

Everyone held their breath. Had the professor found another fragment of bone?

At last the professor put down the glass and beamed up at all of them. 'This is definitely a piece of very ancient bone indeed,' he said excitedly. 'The tides must have washed away many layers of sand and left the skeleton close to the surface.' He stood up with a broad smile on his kindly face. 'I think we've made a find, Quentin! I need to get up to London and get a team organised right away.'

Everyone trooped back to Kirrin Cottage and Professor Ward went into Father's study to make some important telephone calls.

'We're not going to have all the other diggers staying here as well, are we, Mummy?' asked George in horror.

'No, of course not,' said her mother. 'They'll stay at a hotel in the nearest town.'

'That's good,' said George with a sigh of relief.

'Why don't you take Jack to see your tree-house?' said Mother, while they were waiting for the professor to finish his calls. 'I'm sure Father and Professor Ward will be in the study for hours discussing ideas.'

'Oh, all right,' said George, looking round for Jack. But the boy was nowhere to be seen. He had tramped back to Kirrin Cottage with everyone, then disappeared.

'I saw him go outside and into the garden shed,' said Joanna.

'The shed?' exclaimed George. 'What on earth is he doing in there?'

'I've no idea,' said Joanna from where she was standing with a big pile of ironing.

'Go and see, there's a good girl,' said George's

mother. 'I'm sure he'll be glad of your company.'

'I don't know why you think that, Mummy,' said George. 'He doesn't like me one little bit.'

'Well go anyway,' insisted her mother patiently. 'Show him your tree-house. He's bound to like it . . . and be nice to him!' she added.

'Very well,' said George scowling. 'Come on, Timmy.'

Down the garden path the two went. The potting shed door was open and inside, Jack was fiddling around with something.

'What are you doing?' asked George curiously, standing in the doorway, watching.

Jack turned round, looking rather guilty. 'Nothing,' he said.

'Yes, you are,' insisted George, going in and seeing the boy had been examining an old clock her mother had put out for the jumble sale. 'That's my mother's clock, you know.'

'It's broken,' said Jack.

'We know that, silly,' said George 'That's why it's going to the jumble sale.'

'I could mend it,' said Jack. 'I'm awfully good at mending things.'

'You can if you like,' said George, shrugging. 'But I'm supposed to be showing you my tree-house.'

'Tree-house?' said Jack, pulling a face. 'Oh . . . I don't like things like that.' He opened the back of the clock and peered inside. 'I'm scared of heights.'

George gave an irritated sigh. Jack was a very peculiar boy indeed. How could anyone *not* like tree-houses?

8

A secret

'I suppose you don't like swimming or sailing either, then,' said George scornfully when Jack told her he didn't like tree-houses.

'No,' said Jack, poking a small screwdriver into the back of the old clock he had been examining. 'I hate them. I like reading and making and mending things.'

'Well, please yourself,' said George, going out and leaving Jack to his own devices.

George fetched Timothy's ball and took him down the garden to play. He had become very good at fetching a ball and soon brought it back when she threw it as far as she could. He barked excitedly and ran round in circles waiting for her to throw it again. He never seemed to get tired of the game.

'Can I have a go?' asked a voice behind her ten minutes later.

George turned round. Jack was standing there. 'I thought you were mending the clock,' said George.

'I've done it,' said Jack.

George stared at him, screwing up her nose. 'You can't have,' she said. 'It's been broken for ages. How could you mend it so quickly?'

'I told you I was good at mending things,' said Jack. 'I've taken it indoors and put it on the kitchen table.'

'Oh,' said George, rather taken aback. Jack might be a strange kind of boy but it looked as if he was awfully clever all the same.

Reluctantly she let Jack throw the ball for Timothy two or three times. Jack enjoyed the game. He seemed to have quite forgotten that being out in the sun was bad for him.

'You'd better look at the tree-house or Mummy will think I haven't let you see it,' said George, annoyed because Timothy was enjoying his game with the boy.

'All right, then,' said Jack, sighing as if tree-houses were the most boring things in the world instead of one of the best.

George stood underneath the tall old apple tree and pointed upwards. 'Up there,' she said. 'I made most of it myself although William, Joanna's husband, gave me that big wooden box.' The box was nailed to several wooden boards. George had heaved the boards up into the tree and nailed them to a thick branch. The house was rather ramshackle but George thought it was great fun. The only thing that spoiled it was that Timothy was unable to play up there with her. He just sat underneath and whined all the time.

George went to get the ladder from behind

the tree. 'Do you want to go up?' she asked.

'Not likely,' said Jack. 'It looks a bit of a shambles to me,' he added, staring at the house. 'If you had a strong gale it would blow down.'

'No, it wouldn't. We've had lots of gales and it's still there,' said George indignantly.

How dare he be rude about her wonderful tree-house! She was very proud of it. She didn't care that it was a bit lopsided and ramshackle. It was still the best tree-house in the world.

'What does Timmy think of it?' asked Jack.

'He doesn't think anything,' admitted George. 'I can't get him up there.'

Jack made a face and turned away. It was obvious he didn't think much of the tree-house at all. For one thing it was much too high up. For another it looked as if it might collapse at any minute. If you were going to build something, thought Jack, you should jolly well do it properly.

George's mother came out of the back door and through the garden to find them. 'George, dear,' she said. 'Was it you who put that old clock in the kitchen?'

'No,' said George, pointing rather rudely at Jack. 'It was *him*. He's mended it.' Although she didn't like the boy she was very fair and honest and always told the truth.

Her mother turned to Jack. 'Jack! It's going again, ticking away merrily as if it had never stopped. You're a wonder.'

'Thanks,' said Jack. 'I'm good at things like that.'

George's mother smiled broadly and gave the boy a quick hug. 'Oh, Jack, that's marvellous! I'm very fond of the old clock but I really thought it would never go again. Thank you very much.'

Jack went bright red and looked down at his feet. 'That's all right,' he mumbled.

George wasn't very pleased that her mother had hugged Jack. She didn't like her mother being fond of him any more than she liked Timothy being his friend.

Just then they heard Professor Ward's voice calling them from the house and George's mother hurried back indoors to see what he wanted.

George and Jack followed more slowly. Half-way indoors Jack bent and picked Timothy up. 'I wish I had a dog for a friend,' he said wistfully. 'I've always wanted one but we live in a flat and there's nowhere for a dog to run and play.'

George quickly took Timothy from his arms. 'Well, you're not having mine,' she said haughtily and hurried on ahead.

When tea-time came, Joanna laid out fresh egg and cress sandwiches, a bowl of fresh strawberries, a jug of cream, a huge ginger cake and some chocolate biscuits on a small table by the French windows.

'Ah, Jack,' said the professor as he and George's mother came in for tea. 'I hear you've mended Fanny's clock.'

'It was easy,' said Jack, lolling in the chair.

'He's very clever with his hands,' said the professor. 'He's always inventing things.'

'Inventing things? Well, then, Jack,' said George's mother. 'I've got a little task for you.'

'What kind of a task?' asked Jack, sitting up and taking notice.

'Well, the birds are eating the tops of my vegetables,' she explained. 'I've hung all sorts of things round my vegetable patch but they take no notice. No notice at all.'

'Oh,' said Jack. 'Do you want me to invent something that will scare them away, then?'

'Oh, yes please,' exclaimed George's mother. 'It would be lovely if you could.'

'I'm sure I'll be able to,' said Jack, helping himself to two sandwiches. He looked pleased George's mother had asked him. At least it would stop him being bored.

George felt furious. How dare her mother ask this boy to make a bird scarer! *She* was as good as any boy. *She* could easily have made one. She glared at her mother. But her mother was used to such scowls from her short-tempered daughter and ignored her.

'You can do it while I'm in London,' said Professor Ward. 'I'm going to recruit my team and I've invited Fanny and Quentin to come and stay with your mother and I for the night so we can go on an outing to the theatre.'

'I haven't got to go with you, have I?' asked George, hating the thought of all that traffic and noise and no views of the sea and the moors from the windows of their flat.

'No, dear,' said her mother. 'You're going to stay here with Jack. Joanna is going to look after you both.'

'With Jack?' said George, sounding horrified.

'Yes,' said the professor. 'It'll do him good to spend some time by the sea.'

'Does he have to stay, Mummy?' asked George rather rudely. 'Timmy and I will be perfectly all right on our own.'

Timothy barked and went over to Jack as he held out a crust from his sandwich. The puppy wolfed it down then begged for another piece.

George scowled and took a large bite of ginger cake. But even *that* didn't make her feel better! The thought of Jack staying at Kirrin Cottage was really too much to bear!

George's mother sighed. 'George, it really will be nice for you to have Jack here!'

'Yes, Mummy,' said George, still in a huff.

'Wuff,' said Timothy, then lay down as George frowned at him. He stared at her with his head between his shaggy front paws. He quite liked this Jack boy. Especially as he had given him almost a whole sandwich.

'Do I have to stay, Dad?' asked Jack. He obviously didn't like the thought of staying at Kirrin Cottage much either.

'Yes, certainly, you do,' said his father, the professor. 'It will be good for you to get some fresh, country air for a change.'

'You can go swimming and sailing with George,' said her mother. 'And I'm sure she'll row you across to the island.'

'He doesn't like the sea,' said George sulkily.

'Now there's something very important I must tell both of you before I go,' said the professor. 'I'd like you both to keep our discovery a secret. If anyone finds out, we could have hordes of people down here looking for more bones.'

'We won't tell anyone,' promised George. 'Will we, Jack?'

'No,' mumbled Jack, still looking fed up.

'And also,' continued his father. 'Rival professors would dearly like to get their hands on the skeleton. It's an unknown species and it'll be very valuable. So please don't mention it to anyone.'

George felt rather thrilled at this cloak and dagger kind of secret. 'Do you hear that, Timmy?' she whispered in the puppy's ear. 'We *love* keeping secrets, don't we?'

'Wurf,' said Timothy softly. 'Wurf, wurf!'

9

Jack makes a mistake

The following day dawned bright and sunny. George's father and mother and Professor Ward caught the early morning train to London, leaving George and Jack in Joanna's care. The kindly woman often stayed to look after George while her parents went away.

Joanna was in the kitchen cooking breakfast

and humming merrily to herself as the little girl came down the stairs.

The delicious smell of bacon and eggs wafted from the frying pan. George couldn't help her mouth watering.

'Fresh country bacon and farm eggs,' said Joanna when Jack came through the door and she saw him eyeing the frying pan too. 'Not like those things you get in the city. No taste to them at all. Now, you two, what are you going to do with yourselves today?'

'I need to buy some things for the bird scarer,' replied Jack. 'Is there a shop in the village?'

'Oh, yes, dear,' said Joanna. 'Mrs Wood's post-office stores. She sells everything from tintacks to tinned tomatoes.'

'Thank you,' said Jack. 'I'll go after breakfast.'

'Are you going to show Jack how to get there?' Joanna asked George, placing a large plate of sizzling bacon and eggs in front of her.

'If he wants me to,' said George, tucking in.

'Can we catch the bus?' asked Jack.

'Don't be silly,' said George. 'We walk!'

'Walk?' said Jack, looking rather horrified. 'I hope it isn't far. It's jolly hot again today.'

'Of course it's not far,' said George scornfully. 'Timmy and I go there all the time, don't we, Tim? It's a lovely walk across the moor.'

'Wuff,' said Timothy, sitting at Jack's feet and gazing up at him hopefully. The smell of fried bacon really was the most delicious smell in the world.

'Oh well,' said Jack, pulling a face. 'If there isn't a bus I suppose we'll *have* to.'

After breakfast George, Timmy and Jack went along the path that led over the moor to the village. Jack puffed and panted as they ambled along. The sun blazed down from a wonderful blue sky and in the distance they could hear a skylark, its song rising and falling on the morning air.

George was striding on ahead with Timmy.

'Wait for me,' puffed Jack, stumbling a little. 'Phew,' he said as they waited for him to catch up. 'I'm not used to walking everywhere.'

By the time they reached the end of the path,

Jack was very red in the face. George and Timothy hadn't slowed down at all and he was very relieved when they came to the gentle slope that led to the village.

George lagged behind a little. She hated shopping and would much rather play with Timothy and watch the fishing fleet sail out from the little harbour. 'You go on,' she said to Jack. 'I'm going to have a game with Timmy on the beach. Just carry on along the street and you'll soon come to the shop.'

'Righty-ho,' said Jack, hurrying off.

George and Timothy ran along the harbour wall and jumped down on to the pebbles. George found an old shoe that had been washed up by the tide and soon they were having a grand game.

'Come on, Timmy,' George said a while later when they had finished their games and sat for a while watching the fishing fleet. 'We'd better go and see if Jack's finished his shopping.'

When they reached the post-office stores, George could see through the window that Jack had his arms full of all sorts of things. String, sheets of cardboard, glue, jars of poster paint, a roll of tin foil. George couldn't think what he was going to do with them all.

As she went in, Jack was talking to a tall, scruffy-looking boy of about fifteen. He was a stranger in the village.

'I live in London too,' said Jack.

'Are you on holiday here, then?' asked the boy.

'Oh, no, I'm here with my father. He's a professor, you know,' answered Jack, obviously trying to impress the older boy.

'A professor, eh?' remarked the youth, laughing in rather a rough way. 'What's he doing in a boring place like this, then?'

Boring? thought George angrily. How dare this horrid youth call Kirrin boring! It was the most beautiful place in the world.

She was just about to go and tell the boy what she thought of him when she heard Jack reply. 'Yes, it is rather, isn't it?' said Jack. 'But my father's found some extremely rare and valuable prehistoric bones down in the bay, you see.'

'Valuable?' said the youth, raising his thick, dark eyebrows in surprise.

'Yes,' said Jack, lowering his voice a little. 'They were behind a big pointed rock. He—'

But Jack didn't get any further. George marched up to him. She grabbed his arm angrily and pulled him away from the youth.

'For goodness sake, Jack!' she hissed from between clenched teeth. 'You're not supposed

to tell anyone, remember?' She dragged him to one side. Timothy barked excitedly, thinking they were playing a game of some sort.

'Be quiet, Timmy!' commanded George sternly and the little dog quietened down at once.

'That boy was bragging about his dad being a rich and important businessman so I thought I'd tell him about *my* father,' said Jack, shaking George's hand off.

'Well you shouldn't have done,' said George, still feeling very angry indeed. 'Just wait until I tell your father that you've spoiled his secret!'

'Please don't tell my dad,' wailed Jack when he had paid for his things and they were outside. 'He'll be awfully angry. I'm sure that boy and his father wouldn't be interested in old bones.'

'I hope not, for your sake!' said George, striding off.

'Please . . .!' panted Jack, catching up with her. 'Please don't tell him. I'm terribly sorry.'

'All right, I won't tell your father,' said George, giving a sigh and calming down a little. 'But I won't be friends with someone who can't keep a secret!'

She strode off again at a fine old pace and Jack didn't catch up with her until they reached the gate of Kirrin Cottage. 'Come on, Timmy, let's go for a swim,' she said, so angry that she was determined not to speak to Jack again.

'Wuff,' said Timothy. A swim! What a lovely idea on such a hot and muggy day.

George didn't plan to see Jack for the rest of the day. She decided to ask Joanna to pack her and Timothy a picnic so they could spend the whole afternoon on the beach.

'Come on, Timmy,' she called when Joanna had got everything ready and she had fetched her swimming things from her room.

Timothy was outside exploring Mother's flower-beds. He poked his dear little black nose out from between the delphiniums when he heard his mistress calling him.

'Oh, Timmy!' cried George. 'Come out at

once, Mummy will be so cross if you break her flowers!'

'Wuff,' said Timothy, coming out and standing in front of her with his pink tongue lolling out. Exploring flower-beds was hot work indeed. He sniffed the air. He could smell another picnic. Good-oh!

'Come on,' laughed George. 'At least you can't get up to mischief on the beach.'

Halfway along the garden path, George heard a clattering and banging sound. She turned round and saw the most peculiar sight. Jack had his head in the dustbin and was rummaging around in the rubbish. 'What *is* that boy doing now?' she asked Timothy in rather a puzzled voice.

Timothy gave a little whine as if to say he didn't have a clue.

'Oh well, I don't really care *what* he's doing,' said George with a shrug as they went through the gate. 'At least he doesn't want to come on our picnic. Thank goodness!'

Timothy bounded on ahead as George made her way along the narrow path to the beach.

When Timothy came to the place where it sloped gently downwards he suddenly stopped and stared, his ears pricked up and his tail quivering.

'What's wrong, Tim?' called George, running to catch up with him.

A low growl came from Timothy's throat and she saw what he was staring at. Two people were walking along the beach, stopping now and then to pick up pieces of driftwood, examine them, then throw them into the sea.

'Oh, blow!' exclaimed George, her hand on Timothy's collar to stop him bounding off to bark at the strangers. 'I hate it when there are other people about. Let's wait until they've gone, shall we?'

'Wuff,' said Timothy, rather sorrowfully. He would have liked to run up to the people and bark until they went away so he and George could have the bay to themselves straightaway. He had smelled the delicious things Joanna had put in the picnic bag and his mouth was watering.

George sat down, hidden behind a tussock of

grass and pulled Timothy down beside her.

It wasn't long before the two people began to make their way up the cliff path and disappeared out of sight.

'Thank goodness!' said George, heaving a sigh of relief. 'The coast's clear now, Timmy. Come on, race you to the sea!'

She jumped up and raced down the slope on to the sand. Timothy barked excitedly and bounced along beside her.

They spent the afternoon playing on the beach and eating the delicious picnic Joanna had made for them. George had a lovely swim while Timothy splashed about in the shallows, barking at the little wavelets and generally enjoying himself.

When they returned to Kirrin Cottage Jack was nowhere to be seen but George heard noises coming from the garden shed and went to investigate.

Jack was in there, hammering and banging.

'He must be making Mummy's bird scarer,' said George, standing on tiptoe to try to peep in the window to see what he was doing. But the glass was too dirty to see through so she gave up and went on indoors.

Jack didn't come out of the shed until it was time for the evening meal. George was still too angry with him for betraying their secret to ask if he had finished the scarer, even though she was quite curious to see what it looked like.

That evening the fine, muggy weather gave way to a dark and thundery sky.

'There's going to be a storm,' said George, looking out of the window after they had eaten their evening meal.

Jack was lolling in the armchair reading one of George's father's science books. George preferred adventure stories and tales of pirates and smugglers and boys doing brave deeds. Her bookcase was full of them.

'A storm?' said Jack, looking faintly alarmed. 'How do you know?'

'The wind has swung round,' said George. 'And there are white horses in the bay.'

Jack stared out of the window at the sea.

'Where? I can't see any horses,' he said.

'It means the sea is choppy and the waves have got white tops on them, silly,' said George scornfully. 'I love storms, don't you?'

'No,' said Jack. 'I hate them.'

'Oh, you would!' said George. 'You're such a baby!'

'No, I'm not,' said Jack, going back to his book and not saying another word to her all the evening.

George went to bed early, leaving Jack still reading in the lounge. She put Timothy down on his blanket in the kitchen as usual.

'I'll come and get you later when Joanna has gone to bed,' she whispered in his ear.

George's father didn't allow dogs on beds so it was a tremendous secret that Timothy slept in George's room each night. George made sure she got up early each morning, slipped silently down the stairs and put Timothy back in the kitchen before anyone else was up so she never had to confess he had been in her room.

Timothy settled down, turning round and round to make himself a little nest while he waited for George to come back for him. Though he was a very brave puppy, he wasn't at all sure he liked the sound of a storm. The sooner he was up the stairs with George the better!

10

Storm!

It was late when the storm broke. Joanna and Jack had been in bed for ages and George had already tiptoed down and brought Timothy up from the kitchen.

The little girl and her dog sat on the bed watching the lightning flash through her small side window that overlooked the sea.

'Oh, Timmy!' said George, her heart thudding with excitement as the whole horizon was lit up. 'Isn't it thrilling!'

'Wurf,' said Timothy although he wasn't *quite* sure he really liked all the banging and crashing that was going on outside.

Rain lashed the eaves and the wind roared round the roof of the house. Gigantic waves were smashing on the shore in a tumble of white foam. George loved it. It sounded like a fierce battle going on, with swords clashing and horses' hooves thundering.

Each time the lightning burst across the dark sky, Kirrin Island and the castle were lit up for an instant. They looked more mysterious and exciting than ever.

Suddenly, in-between crashes, there was a knock at George's door.

'Oh, blow, it's Joanna! Timmy! Quick, hide!' whispered George, stuffing Timothy rapidly under the bedcovers. If the housekeeper saw him she would be bound to tell Father!

But it wasn't Joanna. When George opened the door Jack was standing there, shivering and looking very scared indeed.

'I w-w-wondered if I could come and sit in your room for a while,' stuttered the boy.

'What on earth for?' exclaimed George, scowling.

'I-I'm scared we'll be struck by lightning,' confessed Jack.

'Oh, for goodness sake!' said George impatiently. 'Of course we won't.'

'We're the only house for miles around,' said Jack, still shivering. 'And lightning is attracted to high places, so we could be.'

'Well, sitting in my bedroom won't stop it, then, will it?' hissed George.

'N-no,' admitted Jack. 'Sh-shall I go back to my room, then?'

George suddenly felt sorry him. She felt a little guilty too. She had told Mother she would try to be nice to him but she hadn't really made any effort at all.

'Oh, come in, then, if you must,' she said impatiently.

'Th-thank you,' said Jack. 'I didn't like to wake Joanna. She'd think I was an awful baby.'

'Well, you are,' said George. 'There's really nothing to be scared of. Look, come over to the window and watch the lightning, it's thrilling!'

'No, thanks,' said Jack, sounding just a little braver now. 'I'll just sit here on the bed.'

He sat down heavily on the side of George's bed. Suddenly there was a yowl and Jack jumped up again as if he had sat on a pin.

'Oh, my goodness!' cried the startled boy as

Timothy scrambled out from under the covers, his tail wagging nineteen to the dozen. He ran round the room jumping up first at George, then at Jack. 'Timmy!' he exclaimed. 'Are you scared of storms too? Is that why you're hiding?'

'No, of course he isn't,' said George impatiently. 'He's the bravest dog that ever lived. And if you tell anyone you've seen him here I'll tell your father about that boy in the village shop!'

'Of course I won't tell anyone,' said Jack, making a fuss of the puppy. 'Isn't he supposed to be here then?'

'No,' confessed George, telling Jack where Timothy was really supposed to sleep.

'What fun!' said Jack, grinning. 'I wish I had a dog to sleep on *my* bed.'

'Why *aren't* you allowed to have one?' asked George curiously. She forgot all about the storm for a minute and turned from the window. She sat down beside Jack and Timothy.

'We haven't got a garden or anything,' explained Jack. 'It wouldn't be fair to have a dog if there's no garden for him to play in.'

'No garden!' exclaimed George. 'How perfectly horrid.'

'It's quite nice where I live, actually,' said Jack. 'But we're not allowed to have pets.' He stroked Timothy and tickled him behind the ear. 'Still, I can pretend Timmy is mine while I'm here, can't I?'

'No, you jolly well can't,' said George indignantly. 'I'm sorry, but no-one can *pretend* to have Timmy. He's mine.'

Jack jumped as a bolt of lightning flashed very close by. Soon after, an enormously loud clap of thunder shook the whole house.

George ran to the window. 'For goodness sake come and look, Jack! You can't be a baby all your life.'

'Oh, all right,' said Jack, suddenly feeling rather bold. He got up from the bed and went cautiously to the window. 'I suppose if you and Timmy aren't scared of thunder and lightning there's no reason why I should be either.'

'That's right,' said George. 'You're just being silly. This house is very old, you know. There have probably been millions of storms since it was built so there's really nothing to worry about.'

Just as Jack reached the window there was a dazzling flash of lightning and the whole beach was lit up.

George gasped. There was someone down there! Two figures, one smaller than the other, were hurrying along the sand carrying heavy spades and sacks across their shoulders.

'Did you see that, Jack?' she cried, turning to him in horror.

Jack *had* seen them. 'They were going towards Needle Rock,' said the boy, sounding shocked. 'And one of them looked like that boy I was talking to in the shop!'

Then George suddenly realized something. The two figures were the same people she had seen that afternoon, picking things up off the beach and throwing them into the water. It must have been the boy and his father looking for signs of the dinosaur bones!

'I bet they're going to dig for the bones,' she cried in horror.

'What would someone like that want old bones for?' asked Jack dubiously.

'To sell for money, of course, stupid!' said George.

'But he told me his father was rich and important,' said Jack.

'He was probably lying,' said George, frowning. 'What on earth are we going to do?'

'Supposing they do find the rest of them,' wailed Jack, looking very worried indeed. 'My dad will be absolutely furious. He'll never trust me again!'

'Well there's only one thing we *can* do,' said George, suddenly feeling quite sorry for Jack. It really was jolly bad luck to have let the secret slip to just the wrong sort of person. 'We'll have to go down there and see what they're up to!'

'We-we can't possibly go *outside*,' stuttered Jack, looking scared again. 'We could get struck by lightning!'

'Well, we'll have to if we're going to save those bones, *and* save you from getting into lots of trouble,' said George determinedly.

Jack shook his head. 'I c-can't,' he stammered. 'I'm too frightened.'

'Oh, for goodness sake go back to bed, then!' said George. 'Timmy and I will just have to go on our own, that's all!'

Jack climbed off her bed and slipped out of the door looking rather shamefaced. He padded along the corridor to his room and closed the door quietly. There was nothing else for it. George and Timothy would have to go out in the storm on their own.

11

Adventures in the night

'Wretched boy,' muttered George, still fuming about Jack as she flung on her trousers and a thick jumper over her pyjamas. She waggled her finger at Timothy. 'Now *don't* make a noise, Timmy. If you wake Joanna I'll be very angry!'

Timothy gave a very quiet little 'wuff' just to show he had heard what she said. This was very exciting! A walk in the dark! He was not at all sure what his little mistress was up to but he had a feeling that it was going to be something absolutely thrilling.

George put her finger to her lips as she crept along the landing past Joanna's bedroom.

She stopped for a moment and listened outside the door. She could hear Joanna's gentle snores and heaved a big sigh of relief. If the thunder hadn't woken her up then it wasn't likely she would hear them creeping down the stairs.

There was no sound from Jack's room either.

'I bet he's hiding under the covers,' she whispered to Timothy as they crept by. 'What a coward!'

Downstairs, George got her mackintosh from the hallstand and slipped her feet into her wellington boots.

'Stay close to me, Timmy,' she hissed as they crept through the kitchen and out of the back door.

Outside, the wind was so strong it almost took away George's breath as she closed the back door softly and set off down the path.

Through the gate they went, on to the track that led down to the beach. George had been along the path hundreds of times and could find her way easily even on the darkest of nights.

The rain stung her face like needles and it wasn't long before Timothy's coat was very wet indeed. Overhead, the lightning flashed and the thunder roared. The storm didn't seem to be abating one bit.

The puppy kept very close to George's feet as she sped along the track and down towards the shore. The rain had made it rather slippery and once or twice she almost lost her balance.

They battled their way on to the beach where the waves were crashing on the shore in a torrent of white foam. Black thunder clouds scudded madly across the sky. George's eyes strained through the darkness to see the two figures. She had her little torch in her pocket but did not dare to put it on in case they were seen.

She spotted the two figures as the sky was lit by lightning once more. They were digging behind Needle Rock. It was certain now. They were trying to find the dinosaur bones!

The two adventurers crept towards them, keeping as close to the cliff base as they could. The wind whipped at George's dark curls and tore at her mackintosh. Her eyes and nose were full of salty spray and Timothy looked just like a drowned rat. He had to keep shaking his head as the water dripped into his eyes and he couldn't see where he was going.

The little dog was not at all sure he liked being out in the dead of night in such a terrible storm after all, even though he knew he had to protect his mistress from any danger that might come their way.

'This way!' whispered George, and Timothy followed her into the shelter of a large rock some way from where the robbers were still digging as hard as they could. 'We can spy on them from here!'

George crouched down with Timmy beside her, her heart thudding like mad. She put her hand on the little dog's head so he would know he wasn't allowed to growl and bark. The storm was very noisy but if the intruders *did* hear him the two of them would be in *real* trouble.

'It *is* that boy from the village shop, Timmy!' hissed George. 'And an older man. I bet it's his father. They look like real villains to me!'

She was desperately racking her brains for ideas. She had to find a way to stop them finding the bones without giving herself and Timothy away.

As they watched, the storm at last began to

abate. The thunder rolled away out to sea and the lightning flashes grew further and further apart. The two figures threw back the hoods of their mackintoshes and begin to dig even harder. Suddenly the youth bent down and picked something up. There was a flash of torchlight that revealed a large bone just like the one Timothy had dug up.

The boy's voice came towards them. 'This looks like one, Dad. There you are, what did I tell you!'

'Oh, blow!' exclaimed George in a whisper. 'They've found one. We've got to stop them, Timmy. We've just got to!'

Just then, Timothy gave a low, warning growl and, to her horror, she heard footsteps crunching on the sand behind her. Suddenly someone grabbed her from behind, putting their hand over her mouth. She tried to scream and yell but the hand was clamped so tightly she couldn't make a sound.

Her heart leaped with fear. Did the two robbers have an accomplice who had discovered her spying on them?

Then a voice hissed in her ear.

'It's all right, George, it's only me, don't make a noise.'

Her arms were released and she spun round. Jack was standing behind her looking very wet and bedraggled and rather sheepish.

'I couldn't let you come on your own after all,' he explained, shivering. 'I decided I'd risk getting struck by lightning and I didn't want you to call out in surprise when I turned up.'

He bent down and gave Timothy a quick stroke. The puppy licked his hand as if to say 'I'm really glad you're here!'

George scowled, angry she had allowed herself to be frightened. 'You scared me!' she whispered furiously.

'Sorry,' said Jack.

'Never mind,' said George, suddenly realizing exactly how brave Jack had been to put aside his fear of the storm and come out to help her. 'They've found a bone, I'm afraid. I saw it by the light of their torch.'

'Oh, blow!' said Jack. 'What are we going to do?'

'We've got to stop them but I've no idea how,' whispered George, shaking her head.

They crouched down behind the rock, watching the two villains at work. They were digging a very deep hole in the sand. Every now and then one of them pulled something out and they both examined it by torchlight, then put it into one of their sacks.

If George and Jack didn't hurry up and think of something quickly, the whole skeleton might soon be uncovered!

Suddenly Jack pulled George's arm and made her stand up. 'I've got an idea,' he whispered. 'Come on, let's go back!'

'We can't . . .' began George. 'We've . . .'

But the boy was already hurrying back along the base of the cliff towards the path.

To George's annoyance Timothy ran after him. Afraid he would bark to get her to follow, George ran to catch them up.

Soon, the three were safely back on the cliff path and hurrying towards Kirrin Cottage.

'What on earth are you doing!' cried George

angrily. 'We can't just leave those horrid men to steal all the bones.'

'We're not going to,' said Jack. 'We're going to scare them away.'

'How?' asked George scornfully. 'They're a lot bigger than us!'

'Wait and see,' said Jack mysteriously.

To George's surprise, he led them towards the garden shed and threw open the door.

'You haven't got a torch, I suppose, have you?' he asked when they were inside.

'Of course I have,' said George, pulling her little torch from her pocket. 'I always carry it *and* my penknife and string. You never know when you're going to have an adventure and need things like that.'

'Good,' said Jack, sounding full of admiration. 'Shine it over here.'

George was astonished to see a most peculiar contraption in the corner of the shed. There were empty baked bean tins fished out of the dustbin and washed, pink painted cardboard cones and strips of silver paper and all manner of other things tied on to a long piece of strong string.

'What on earth is *that*?' exclaimed George.

'It's my bird scarer, silly,' said Jack. 'And if my plan works, it will be a thief scarer too!'

12

A terrific plan

George stared at the gadget with her hands on her hips. 'How on earth are we going to scare them with that thing?' she exclaimed scornfully.

Jack quickly explained how the bird scarer worked. A broad grin spread across George's face. If Jack was right, his device would scare away a whole horde of robbers, not just two!

'We could do with a whistle, too,' said Jack, looking thoughtful. 'I don't suppose you've got one, have you?'

'Of course,' said George, taking hers from her pocket. 'I always carry one of those too.'

Jack looked at George in amazement. He was obviously thinking what a remarkable little girl she was. 'Well done,' he said admiringly. 'Right, let's get back down to the beach.'

So the two brave children and the little shaggy dog picked up the extremely strange contraption and set off down the garden path once more.

Timmy ran on ahead, his shaggy tail waving like a banner. Now the storm had rolled away, it was very dark indeed but dogs could see very well in the dark and he was quite happy to lead the way!

George was so used to the path she didn't even hesitate but once or twice Jack stumbled and almost fell over on the slippery, stony track.

They had to be very careful not to let the tin cans rattle together and warn the robbers they were coming.

'Timmy, darling, heel!' hissed George as they hurried down the slope that led to the beach.

Timothy slowed his pace. He was dying to get on with the adventure. He had spotted the robbers too and was absolutely longing to bark and bark until they ran away.

They kept close to the base of the cliff as they crept towards Needle Rock.

The men were still digging furiously. They had balanced their torch on a smaller rock and were working in the beam of light. One of their sacks looked almost full up.

Suddenly their voices echoed towards the crouching children.

'Look at this one, Jim,' grunted the older man. 'It's a real whopper. Should be worth a fortune I reckon.'

The youth hurried over and together they tried to heave an enormous bone from the trench.

'We'll never get it out,' panted the man. 'We'll 'ave to come back for it another time.'

'Don't be daft, Dad,' replied the youth. 'Once they find out we've been 'ere they'll guard the site. It's now or never!' He began hacking away at the sand with his spade.

'Rotten devil!' hissed Jack angrily. 'He'll ruin it. You have to be very careful with these ancient bones.'

'We'd better get started then,' whispered George.

'Right,' agreed Jack.

'I'll creep round the back of the rock,' said George. 'I'll take one end of the scarer with me.

You stay here. We'd both better start together.'

'Right,' said Jack. 'I'll start counting to a hundred when you set off. You do the same and when we get to a hundred we'll begin.'

'Good idea,' whispered George. 'Come on, Timmy, you come with me!'

George held the contraption very close to her chest as she and Timmy crept along in the shadow of the cliff, then across to Needle Rock. She hardly dared to breathe and her heart beat so hard it hurt. She managed to get very close to the men and could hear the crunch of their spades as they dug into the ground.

Timothy was as good as gold. He knew by the tone of his mistress's voice that it was very important to be quiet. He did not know how long he was going to be able to resist barking at the horrible strangers. He just hoped he could hold off until George told him it would be all right.

'Sixty one ... sixty two ... sixty three ...' murmured George to herself as she crouched behind Needle Rock. She breathed a huge, silent sigh of relief. The men had not spotted her or heard a single thing.

'Ninety one ... ninety two ... ninety three ...' George's heart was still beating like a drum. Would their plan work? If it didn't and the men discovered them, then things could get very nasty indeed!

'Ninety nine ... one HUNDRED!'

On the count of a hundred an awful din broke loose over the peaceful Kirrin Bay.

First of all a loud voice boomed across the sand. 'All right, you two, the game's up! You're surrounded, so it's no good trying to get away!'

Then a whistle blew and a very fierce dog began barking madly. Another voice rang out from behind Needle Rock. 'You'd better hand those bones over to us now, you men. You're under arrest!'

There was a rattling and banging sound and a quite deafening whistle screeched out, sounding just like a police whistle.

The villains looked round in horror and fear, dropping their spades in shock.

'It's the police!' exclaimed Jim. 'Come on, Dad, run for it!'

'They've, dogs and all!' yelled Jim's father as they both took to their heels and ran.

'After them, men!' came a loud, deep voice as the two villains sped off along the water's edge, running as fast as they possibly could. The fierce barking followed them and a loud voice called. 'Quick, men! Don't let them get away!'

The two robbers left the sacks, turned and rushed across the sand and up to the base of the cliff. They both began to climb the rocky path, scrambling and slipping dangerously as they went.

The moon came out from behind a cloud just as the men disappeared over the top. Then a car's engine started up and with a roar the two robbers skidded away across the moor towards the road.

Down below, George, Timmy and Jack were staring upwards.

'Hurrah!' shouted George, jumping up and down. 'We've saved the bones. Yippee!'

Jack was jumping up and down too and laughing his head off. 'They really thought the police were here and they were going to be arrested. What brilliant fun!'

'And they thought Timmy was a fierce police dog!' laughed George, bending down and giving Timothy a huge hug and a pat. 'Well done, Timmy. You were marvellous!'

'My scarer was pretty remarkable, don't you think?' asked Jack.

'Terrific!' said George. 'You're jolly clever, you know, Jack.' She picked up one of the cardboard cones and shouted through it. 'All right, you two, the game's up!' Her voice came out, deep and booming, magnified a hundred times by the shape of the cone. She collapsed with laughter again and Jack danced round with Timothy who barked joyfully that their plan had worked so well.

'It was too dark to see their faces but I bet they were scared stiff,' said Jack laughing too.

'Come on,' said George, gathering up the bird scarer. 'We'd better get back before Joanna wakes up and wonders where we've gone.'

'What about the bones?' asked Jack, looking worried. 'We don't want to leave them here, they might come back for them!' He tried to lift one of the sacks but it was so heavy he couldn't even get it off the ground.

'I know,' said George suddenly. 'There's a cave just along the end of the beach. Let's drag them along there and hide them until your father gets home and we can all come and collect them.'

'Jolly good idea,' said Jack.

So, together, George and Jack heaved and dragged the full sack of bones along to the end of the beach and hid it in the cave. Timothy tried to help but only succeeded in tearing a hole in the sack as he grabbed it in his mouth.

'It's all right, thanks, Timmy,' panted Jack. 'I think we can manage without you this time.'

George glanced at him and chuckled. Being with Jack was turning out to be jolly good fun after all!

13

The end of the adventure

It was getting light by the time the two sacks were safely hidden from sight.

George, Timothy and Jack walked back to Kirrin Cottage, laughing and chattering about their adventure. The storm had disappeared and it was going to be a lovely, bright day.

'Your dad will be pleased that the bones are

safe,' said George as they went through the garden gate and down the path to the house.

'Yes,' said Jack, pulling a face. 'But he won't be very pleased when he finds out they only knew the bones were there because *I* gave away the secret.'

They piled the bird scarer back in the shed and went indoors.

Joanna was already up, putting the kettle on for her morning cup of tea. She was very surprised indeed to see them coming through the door.

'My, you three are up early,' she said. 'I wondered where Timmy was. I didn't realize you'd taken him for a walk.'

George glanced at Jack. Should they tell Joanna about their adventure?

But before she could decide whether to or not, Jack blurted it out.

'Some men were trying to steal the bones,' he said without thinking. 'We scared them away.'

'Scared them away?' said Joanna, looking shocked. 'How on earth did you do that?'

So they sat down in the kitchen, sipping mugs

of Joanna's hot chocolate and told her all about it.

'A bird scarer?' she exclaimed. 'How did you frighten those villains with a *bird scarer*?'

'I made cones out of cardboard,' explained Jack. 'And when the wind blows through them they make a strange noise.'

'So we *shouted* through them,' said George, laughing. 'And our voices sounded terrifically loud. They thought lots of police had come to arrest them.'

'There are tins that rattle together and silver paper that flashes in the sunlight,' said Jack. 'It looks as if those things frighten robbers as well as birds.'

'And they thought Timmy was a police dog,' said George. 'Oh, Joanna it was so funny to see them running away from a little puppy!'

'Well, you're all very brave,' said Joanna, wiping her eyes and laughing so much her chin wobbled. 'Your parents are going to be very proud of you, you know.'

'And we're proud of Timmy,' laughed George, giving her darling puppy a big hug.

'He loves adventures just as much as we do.'

'Well, if you're going to have any more,' said Joanna, trying to be stern, 'I hope they won't be in the middle of the night!'

It was lunch-time when George's parents and the professor arrived home. George had been brushing the sand out of Timothy's coat until it shone like gold. Jack had disappeared into the potting shed. There was a lot of hammering and banging coming from inside.

'Has everything been all right?' asked George's mother as she came through the door and put her suitcase down in the hall.

'Oh, yes, fine,' said George, giving her a hug. 'Actually we've had a bit of an adventure.'

'An adventure?' said her father, coming in behind her. 'What *kind* of an adventure?'

'I'll get Jack and we'll tell you all about it,' said George, rushing off to find her friend.

She went into the shed but Jack was nowhere to be seen. Then George spotted him standing beneath the tree-house.

'Everyone's home, Jack,' she called. 'And they want to hear about our adventure.' She stopped in her tracks. There was a rope hanging from the tree with a kind of sling attached to it. What on earth had Jack been inventing now? 'What's that?' she asked, looking very puzzled.

'It's a hoist for Timmy,' explained Jack. 'Look, you put him in this canvas sling I've made out of an old sack, then you go up the ladder and pull it up.'

'He'll bump into the trunk,' said George doubtfully.

'No, look, I've put a wheel at the top to act as a pulley,' said Jack who had overcome his fear of heights and climbed the ladder to put it up there. 'He'll be up in a flash and won't come to any harm at all.'

They tried it out and it worked extremely well.

'Oh, Jack, it's wonderful,' exclaimed George, her eyes shining with joy. 'We can have heaps of fun now. Thanks very much!'

'That's all right,' mumbled Jack, going a bit red in the face.

'And you climbed the ladder too,' said George, suddenly remembering how frightened Jack had been of climbing up high.

Jack shrugged. 'Well, I thought if I could go out in a thundering great storm then I could easily climb up into a silly old apple tree.'

George laughed. 'Well done, Jack. You're braver than any boy I've ever known!'

'Wurf, wurf,' said Timothy, agreeing with his mistress. He loved it up in the tree-house. He could see further than any other dog in the world. What jolly good fun!

'Are you coming indoors to tell us about your adventure?' called George's mother from below. 'We're dying to hear what has happened.'

So, George, Timothy and Jack piled indoors to tell the story of their adventure all over again.

'My word, you two,' said George's father admiringly. 'You were very brave indeed.'

'You mean us *three*,' said George indignantly. 'We couldn't have done it without Timmy!'

'The sacks were too heavy for us to carry so we've hidden them in a cave,' said Jack. 'We'll all go down later to collect them, shall we?'

'We certainly will,' said his father. 'My team are arriving tomorrow. They'll be pleased to hear that some of the job has already been done for them!'

'Well, thank goodness none of you came to any harm and those villains didn't get away with any of the bones,' said George's father.

'Yes,' said Professor Ward. 'I feel sure the whole skeleton is there and it would have been awful if some of it went missing.'

'But how did they know the bones were there

in the first place?' asked George's mother, looking puzzled. 'I thought it was supposed to be a secret.'

'Village gossip, I expect,' said George, hurriedly getting up out of her chair. 'Come on, Jack, let's play in the tree-house.'

'Righty-ho,' said Jack, giving her a grateful glance for not giving him away.

Down the garden they went again. Two children and a little, shaggy, bouncing dog.

George grinned as her friend Jack climbed the ladder and pulled Timothy up on to the platform. Jack was terribly clever. It didn't matter one little bit that he didn't like swimming, or fishing or sailing or things that boys usually like. It was quite enough for him to be awfully brainy!

George climbed the ladder and sat on the platform with her arm round Timothy.

'I hope we're going to have lots more adventures like that, Timmy, darling,' she whispered in his cocked ear, her vivid blue eyes shining with excitement.

'Will you write to me and tell me about them

if you do?' asked Jack rather enviously.

'I'll try,' said George although she wasn't very good at writing letters.

'Thanks,' said Jack. 'That will be fun.'

'Not as much fun as actually having them,' said George, giving Timothy another hug. 'Will it, Timmy, darling?'

'Wuff,' said Timothy, agreeing as usual. Nothing in the world was as much fun as having adventures with George!

Just George 3:
George, Timmy and the Footprint in the Sand

Sue Welford

Someone is on George's island. She and Timmy have discovered a mysterious footprint in the sand. Creeping up on a pair of crooks hiding out, they overhear them planning a robbery. But before George and Timmy can row for help, George is spotted and captured! Can Timmy help her escape?

**Just George 4:
George, Timmy and the Secret in the
Cellar**

Sue Welford

George and Timmy are exploring the barns
at Kirrin Farm when Timmy suddenly
disappears. His barking leads George to a
secret trap-door into a dusty cellar below.
And when George clambers down to him,
she is amazed to discover an old trunk full
of mysterious documents. Could she and
Timmy have just discovered an important
secret?

ORDER FORM

Just George

Sue Welford

0 340 77863 6	1: George, Timmy and the Haunted Cave	£3.50	☐
0 340 77864 4	2: George, Timmy and the Curious Treasure	£3.50	☐

and look out for more Just George titles, coming soon!

0 340 77871 7	3: George, Timmy and the Footprint in the Sand	£3.50	☐
0 340 77876 8	4: George, Timmy and the Secret in the Cellar	£3.50	☐
0 340 77879 2	5: George, Timmy and the Stranger in the Storm	£3.50	☐
0 340 77882 2	6: George, Timmy and the Lighthouse Mystery	£3.50	☐

All Hodder Children's books are available at your local bookshop, or can be ordered direct from the publisher. Just tick the titles you would like and complete the details below. Prices and availability are subject to change without prior notice.

Please enclose a cheque or postal order made payable to *Bookpoint Ltd*, and send to: Hodder Children's Books, 39 Milton Park, Abingdon, OXON OX14 4TD, UK.
Email Address: orders@bookpoint.co.uk

If you would prefer to pay by credit card, our call centre team would be delighted to take your order by telephone. Our direct line *01235 400414* (lines open 9.00 am–6.00 pm Monday to Saturday, 24 hour message answering service). Alternatively you can send a fax on *01235 400454*.

TITLE	FIRST NAME	SURNAME	

ADDRESS	

DAYTIME TEL:	POST CODE

If you would prefer to pay by credit card, please complete:
Please debit my Visa/Access/Diner's Card/American Express (delete as applicable) card no:

Signature .... Expiry Date: ....

If you would NOT like to receive further information on our products please tick the box.   ☐